**Studio Fun International**
An imprint of Printers Row Publishing Group
A division of Readerlink Distribution Services, LLC
10350 Barnes Canyon Road, Suite 100, San Diego, CA 92121
www.studiofun.com

Adapted by Marilyn Easton
Based on the adaptation by Brooke Vitale
Designed by Judy Liu

Printers Row Publishing Group is a division of Readerlink Distribution Services, LLC.
Studio Fun International is a registered trademark of Readerlink Distribution Services, LLC.

All notations of errors or omissions should be addressed to Studio Fun International,
Editorial Department, at the above address.

ISBN: 978-0-7944-4707-6
Manufactured, printed, and assembled in Dongguan, China.
First printing, July 2020. RRD/07/20
24 23 22 21 20  1 2 3 4 5

# Disney

# THE Sorcerer's Apprentice

studio **fun** INTERNATIONAL

Once there was a great sorcerer who knew everything there was to know about magic.

He brewed potions that could make camels talk.

He transformed pebbles into rubies and diamonds.

He made the stars shoot across the sky and burst onto the ground wherever he directed them.

The Sorcerer had a wonderful hat. When he wore his hat, all he had to do was think magic and it would happen.

He could think about a butterfly and it would appear.

But only the Sorcerer knew the magic words that would make it disappear.

The Sorcerer was very busy. He did not have time to tend to his castle and still perform his brilliant magic. So he had a helper.

Mickey did all the work in the castle. He swept the floor.
He chopped the wood. He had many tasks.

But his least favorite task was carrying buckets of water from the fountain into the castle.

The buckets were quite heavy.

Late one evening, the Sorcerer yawned deeply. All of his work had made him very tired. Mickey watched as the Sorcerer cleaned up his workshop, placed his hat on the table, and headed toward the stairs.

Soon Mickey found himself all alone.

He saw the magic hat sitting on the table, faintly glowing.

Mickey tried to walk away, but the temptation was too great.
He had seen the magic the Sorcerer could perform with the hat,
and he longed to have a magic hat of his own.

Mickey looked at the magic hat.

Ever so slowly, he reached for it.

Ever so gently, he took it off the table.

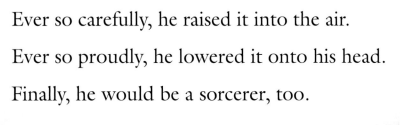

Ever so carefully, he raised it into the air.

Ever so proudly, he lowered it onto his head.

Finally, he would be a sorcerer, too.

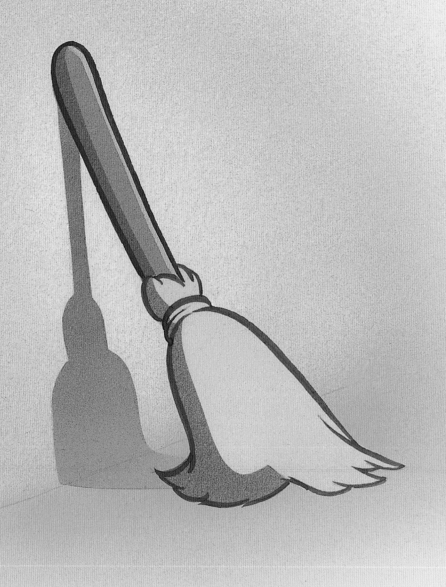

As Mickey peered around the room, his gaze fell on an old broom leaning against the wall.

Suddenly, Mickey knew what his first spell would be.

Mickey did what the Sorcerer always did. He pointed his fingers straight at the broom. At once, the broom began to shake.

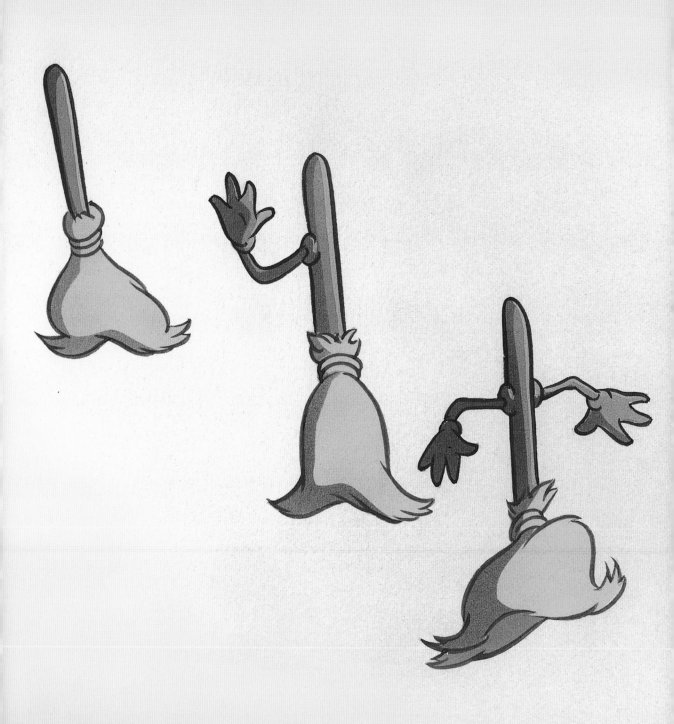

With a flash, the broom leaped forward. Its bristles had parted, turning into two legs.

Mickey pointed at the broom again and it sprouted a right arm, and then a left arm.

Reaching down, the broom picked up two nearby buckets.

Mickey was delighted. Now he would have a helper to do all of his tasks. He would start with the one he liked least—fetching water from the fountain to bring to the castle.

Mickey gestured for the broom to follow him up the steps. The broom did as Mickey commanded.

Mickey led the broom to the fountain and waited for it to fill the buckets. Then Mickey led the broom back down the stairs. Pointing at a large vat, he watched as the broom poured the water inside.

Again and again, the broom marched up the stairs, filled the buckets, and poured the water into the vat.

Mickey danced around the room. Doing magic was easy. He would never have to work again!

But ordering the broom around
had made Mickey tired. He sat down
in the Sorcerer's chair. Waving his hand,
he kept the broom working.

Mickey's eyelids started to feel very heavy. What would be the
harm if he took a quick nap? The broom would keep working while
he slept, and Mickey would wake up to his task being completed.
Soon Mickey fell sound asleep.

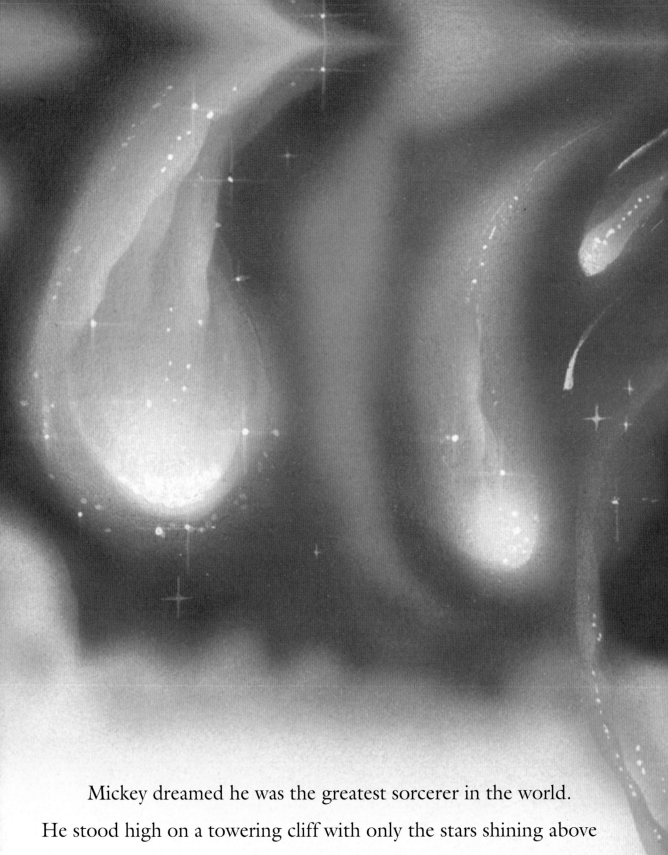

Mickey dreamed he was the greatest sorcerer in the world.
He stood high on a towering cliff with only the stars shining above
him. As he pointed to each star, it burst with light. Mickey gestured
for the stars to swirl across the sky.

It was one of the most beautiful things Mickey had ever seen.

Mickey turned his attention toward the waves gently lapping against the bottom of the cliff.

He swooped his hands high, as if he were scooping the waves out of the water. Soon, the waves crashed all around Mickey. He could almost feel the mist from the waves on his cheeks.

Then, something cold and wet hit Mickey.

It was a splash of water.

Another splash knocked Mickey out of the chair.

Mickey woke up and looked around. There was water everywhere! While he had slept, the broom had continued filling the vat with water. Now it was overflowing and flooding the room.

When Mickey reached the stairs, he found the broom marching down them with two water-filled buckets in its grasp.

Mickey threw out his hands, commanding the broom to stop. But alas, Mickey only knew how to make the magic start. He did not know how to make it stop.

The broom walked right past Mickey.

If Mickey couldn't stop the broom, it would continue filling the buckets and bringing them back to the vat. It would only make the flooding worse.

The broom emptied the buckets into the vat,
along with Mickey.

Mickey climbed out of the overflowing vat and raced after the broom.

But how would he stop it?

Suddenly, Mickey spotted the ax he used to chop the Sorcerer's wood. He grabbed the ax and chopped the broom into bits. Soon there was nothing left but a pile of splinters.

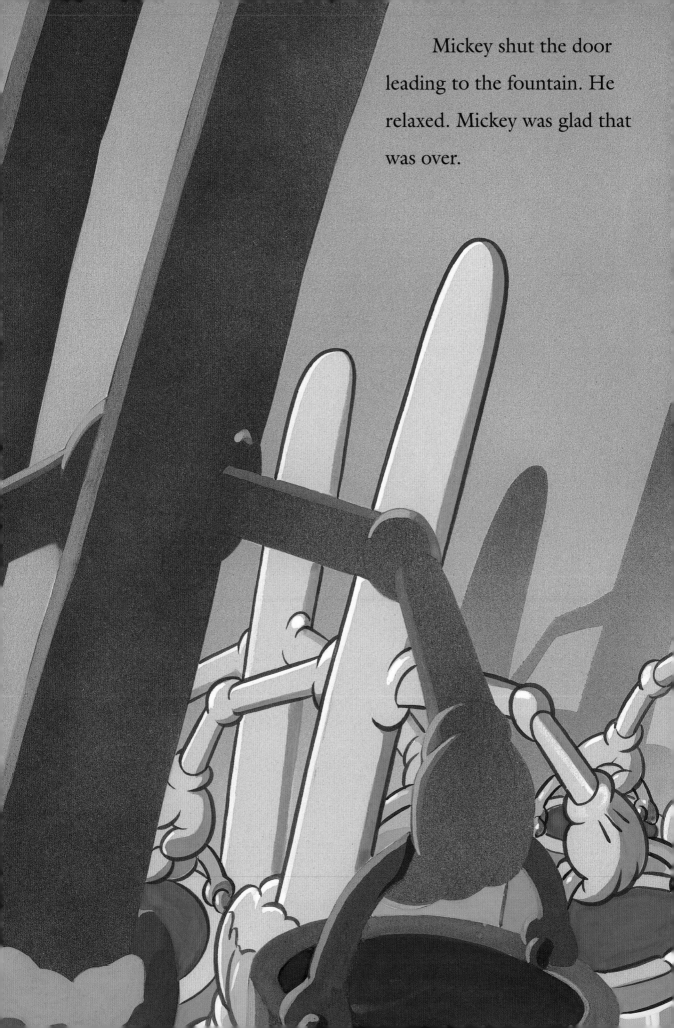

Mickey shut the door leading to the fountain. He relaxed. Mickey was glad that was over.

But it wasn't over.

The bits of wood began to move. Each piece turned into a new broom, and each broom had two new buckets.

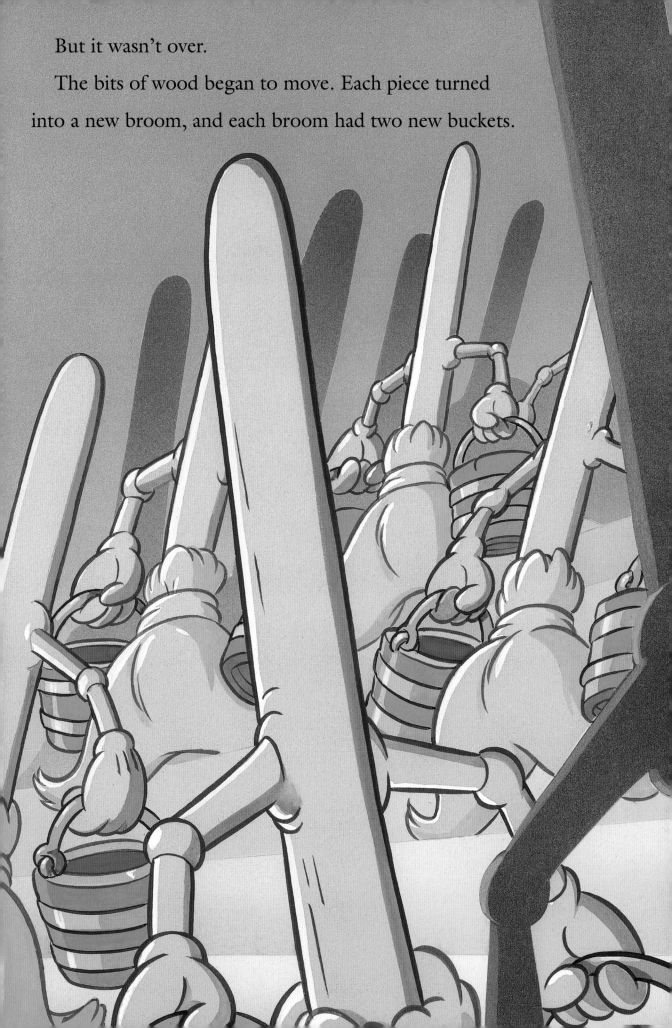

Mickey heard a noise coming from the other side
of the door. He opened it, saw the brooms, and quickly
shut the door.

But he wasn't quick enough. Before he could secure the door, the brooms opened it, their combined strength too powerful for Mickey.

The brooms pushed past Mickey and marched up the stairs. A moment later, the brooms came back down the steps with more water. Mickey tried to hold them back, but it was no use. They walked right over him.

In a great line, they poured more and more water into the vat. The water in the room grew deeper and deeper.

Mickey grabbed a bucket. He started dumping water out of a nearby window. But the brooms were working too quickly. Soon, Mickey was completely underwater.

Mickey swam to the surface, searching for something to keep him above the waves.

The Sorcerer's book of magic floated by. Mickey grabbed it. He turned page after page after page, looking for the magic words that would stop the brooms.

But as the water began to churn, Mickey could no longer read the words.

On a nearby wall, he saw the shadows of the brooms continuing to fill the castle with water.

Then, he was sucked into a great whirlpool.

Mickey hung on to the book as he went around and around in the water, spinning faster and faster.

Suddenly, a bright light filled the room.

The Sorcerer had returned.

Looking at the water covering

his workshop, the Sorcerer knew

at once what Mickey had done.

He raised his arms and waved a great command.

The water parted and began to disappear.

Mickey looked around the room. The Sorcerer was very powerful, even without his wonderful hat.

The Sorcerer frowned down at Mickey, then waved his arms again. The brooms and the buckets disappeared. Soon only Mickey's old broom and buckets remained.

Mickey took off the Sorcerer's hat. Very carefully, he tried to make the magic hat look nice again, straightening the bent top. Then he extended it toward the Sorcerer.

The Sorcerer snatched the hat from Mickey's hand.

Mickey smiled shyly at the Sorcerer. But the Sorcerer did not smile back.

Mickey handed the old broom to the Sorcerer. Then,
he picked up his buckets and headed toward the fountain.
The Sorcerer watched him very closely.

Mickey quickly ran off to do his work. He had learned his lesson: never start something you don't know how to finish.